SHHH! IT'S A SURPRISE!
Scrub-a-Dub-Dub, Rebecca's in the Tub!
Copyright © 2014 by Donna Simard

ISBN: 978-1-4866-0583-5

Word Alive Press
131 Cordite Road, Winnipeg, MB R3W 1S1
www.wordalivepress.ca

WORD ALIVE
—P R E S S—

Library and Archives Canada Cataloguing in Publication

Simard, Donna, 1959-, author
        Shhh! It's a surprise! : scrub-a-dub-dub, Rebecca's in the tub
/ Donna Simard.

(The surprise series)
Issued in print and electronic formats.
ISBN 978-1-4866-0583-5 (pbk.).--ISBN 978-1-4866-0195-0 (pdf).--
ISBN 978-1-4866-0196-7 (html).--ISBN 978-1-4866-0197-4 (epub)

        I. Title. II. Series: Simard, Donna, 1959- . Surprise series.

PS8637.I366S445 2014   jC813'.6   C2014-905693-1
                                                C2014-905694-X

This book belongs to:

_____

To all our grandchildren

Rebecca watched her mother as she turned the tap on the bathtub.

"I don't want a bath!" Rebecca complained.

"If you hurry and climb in the bathtub, we can play a game. We can play the Shhh! It's a Surprise! game," Mother said playfully.

Rebecca loved the animal guessing game. She quickly undressed and climbed into the warm sudsy water. Her mother dumped the bright red bucket of assorted rubber animals into the water.

"Okay, here is your first clue. This animal is very smart."

Rebecca pulled out a brown puppy with big floppy ears. "A puppy is pretty smart."

Mother laughed, "Yes, but this animal is much bigger than a puppy."

She washed Rebecca's red curly hair with sweet-smelling strawberry shampoo. "This animal loves his bath. Sometimes he even takes showers. Like this!" She poured clean water over Rebecca's hair. Gentle giggles filled the room.

"What kind of animal has a shower?"
"Shhh! It's a surprise," Mother teased.

Rebecca frowned as she looked at all of the animals in the tub.

Could it be a lion, a tiger, a monkey or a frog? Hmm.

"Can you guess what this animal does after his bath?" Mother asked.

"What?"

"He covers himself in mud."

"Why would he do that? He will just have to bathe again," said Rebecca.

"He goes in the mud to protect himself from insects and the sunlight," explained Mother.

Rebecca rubbed the cherry soap between her two hands and gently washed her body clean.

"Okay, I'm ready for another clue!" Rebecca said excitedly.

"This animal has very little hair," her mother said.

Rebecca plucked a pig out of the water. "I think it's a pig."

Mother laughed as the soapy water splashed. "No, this animal has wrinkled skin, just like your fingers are getting from staying in the tub too long."

Rebecca looked at her fingers and asked, "Is this animal really old?"

"No," Mother pulled the plug to drain the water out of the tub. "He is wrinkled because that's how God made him."

Rebecca studied each animal as she placed them into the bucket. Could it be a bird, a goat, or a giraffe? "This is a hard guessing game."

"This wild animal can drink more than all the water in your bathtub in one day."

"Wow!" Rebecca exclaimed. "He must be very thirsty. I know... it's a camel!"

"No, it's not a camel." Mother helped Rebecca from the tub and wrapped her in a fluffy orange housecoat. She gently dried her off. "This animal has ears that are much bigger than you, and it can hear very well."

"I know. It's an elephant!" Rebecca squealed in excitement.

"You guessed it! He is the largest animal that lives on land," Mother informed her.

Rebecca put on her pink pajamas. "Look, I have elephants on my pajamas." Rebecca pointed to one elephant on her pajama top and asked, "Why would God give them such funny looking teeth?"

"Oh, those are called tusks. They use them to dig with and to protect themselves."

Rebecca started combing her hair. "I love elephants. Where do they live?" she said.

Mother explained, "Elephants come from faraway places, like Africa, India, and Southeast Asia."

"Can I have a pet elephant?"

"Oh my," Mother chuckled. "Where would we put him?"

Hugging Rebecca close to her, she said, "Elephants have their own special homes just like we do."

"I like my home," Rebecca said. "Elephants are very special, and I'm going to thank God for making them."

Mother kissed Rebecca's forehead and whispered, "I'm going to thank God for making you!"

Interesting Facts about Elephants

- Next time you have a bath look at all of the water in it. Most grown elephants drink more than this in one day. They can drink up to 40 gallons or 150 litres a day.

- Elephants love to roll in the mud, but they love to wash too. They are lucky because they carry their own special hose (trunk) and can take a shower or can spray like a water gun. How fun is that!

- An elephant could carry up to three grown men with its trunk. If those men were to weigh 200 pounds each that is a total of 600 pounds. Wow! That is strong, and that's just with its trunk. They can carry a lot more than that on their backs. You can read books about elephants or check on some websites to see just how much they can carry.

- An elephant is the largest animal that lives on land. They also have the largest ears. Those ears can be 4 feet or 1.2 meters wide. If you lay a child that is four feet tall on the ground and look from the top of his head to the tips of his toes, that would be how wide one ear of an elephant would be.

- The elephant also has the largest teeth of any animal. They are called tusks.

- If you drop a dime, an elephant could pick it up with his trunk. He is very agile and very smart.

- Elephants cannot see very well and are colorblind. This does not make it easier to hide from an elephant. They can hear up to two miles away and have a great sense of smell.

Bibliography

Schindel, John. *Busy Elephants*. Berkeley: Tricycle Press, 2011.

Stewart, Melissa. *Elephants*. Chicago: Children's Press, 2002.

"Elephant." The World Book Encyclopedia, 1988.

www.enature.com

www.nature-wildlife.com

Collect all

The Surprise Series Books!

Book 1: Michael and Dad at the Zoo

ISBN: 978-1-4866-0395-4

Visit the animals at the zoo with Michael and his Dad. At the zoo they play a special game called *Shhh! It's a Surprise.* Play along with them and try and guess which animal is Michael's favorite. Could it be an elephant, a monkey, or a zebra? While playing this game, you will find out that all animals are God's special creations, and that *you* are special too!

Book 3: A Sleepover at Grandma and Grandpa's Farm!

(Coming Soon!)

Join in as Michael and Rebecca go for a sleepover at their Grandparent's farm. Try to guess which animal is Grandpa's favorite! *Shhh! It's a Surprise!*

CPSIA information can be obtained
at www.ICGtesting.com
Printed in the USA
456798LV00003BA/3

9781486605835